# Marisol

Written by Nury Castillo Crawford

Illustrated by Demitrius "Motion" Bullock

1010 PUBLISHING

For information about permission to reproduce selections from this book, email 1010PublishingUS@gmail.com, subject line, "Permission".

Bulk book orders (minimum ten books) can be made by emailing the invoice with tax exempt i.d. to 1010PublishingUS@gmail.com, subject line, "bulk book order".

www.1010Publishing.com

ISBN: 978-1-7344504-1-5

Printed in the United States of America.

# Table of Contents

Preface

Dedication

# Preface

Marisol is a young girl and, like many preteens, has a lot of responsibilities that she doesn't think she deserves. Why can't life just be simple? Why does she have to watch over her tattle-tale sister all of the time? It's just not fair and just when things seem to become almost intolerable, she learns some things may not be as they first appear.

Could it be that there's a silver lining to her everyday struggles?

# Dedication

This story is dedicated to all of the young girls out there. Middle school can be challenging. And as you try to find your way in a new school setting, take each day slowly and remember to laugh. Find a friend or two that you can rely on, sometimes it might be the person you least expect.

This is a reminder that you are enough just the way you are. Life has its ups and downs for sure. Some days are a little bit tougher than others and responsibilities can sometimes be overwhelming.

Hang in there and find your own sunshine!

Love – *Nury*

# Chapter 1
# Dear Diary

As long as I can remember I have kept a journal. You know, something like a diary. That seems a little old fashioned, I'm sure. To me, it's more like my very own therapy. It helps my mind leave reality and think of other things besides my parents' worries and all of the responsibilities that I have as the oldest kid in my family.

September 12

Dear Diary,

So today, as I get off the bus, a blonde-haired boy hands me a folded piece of paper. I look at him and he smiles. I'm really glad he's not saying anything to me since I don't really know him. He's kinda cute though, in a gringo kind of way. School was uninteresting to me. It kinda seems easy and the kids are not very interested in what's going on in class. It must be the teacher. She's nice, but she really is boring! In class, I mostly just doodle on my folders, notebooks and sometimes even on my hands. Although, I heard you can get ink poison that way. I also daydream a lot, mostly about places I read about and want to visit. I've learned about some amazing places from the books I borrowed from the public library.

Marisol

*What are you doing? Let me see what you're writing*", says la chismosa, Elena.

She's always asking me what I'm doing, why I'm doing it and is basically all in my business. She's "la chismosa" because the second she thinks it's not perfectly okay for me to do whatever it is I'm doing, she runs and tells Mami. So, just like clockwork, I hear her tell mom I'm writing secrets in a notebook. Thank goodness I hear Mami tell her, *"You shouldn't tattle on your sister. That's not what sisters should do."*

There, chismosa! Listen to Mami and mind your own, I say in my head.

When Elena walks back into our room - yeah, we share a bedroom with two twin beds -I give her a side-eye look and shake my head. She tries to pretend to not know why I'm giving her that look. She sits on her bed and gets her notebook out too, except she likes to draw. She doesn't really write a lot. She's actually pretty good at drawing stuff. I jump on my neatly made bed and open up my current book. I picked it up from the school library. I spend a lot of time reading since there's not much else I can do. My dad is pretty strict and says, *"no eres animal no puedes estar en la calle"*, so I get to stay home. I guess I could stay after school like the gringitos for a club or sport, but we don't have money for that. And who would pick me up? We only have one car right now. Besides, I like my room. Well, my shared room.

There's my side and then there's Elena's side. Her side looks like a tornado has hit it. There's clothes and her school stuff is everywhere.  My side is neat and I dust often. I like order and clearly, she does not. One day I will have my very own room, a neat room with a humongous bed and pretty curtains that match the comforter, maybe even an accent chair...Well a girl can dream right?

I hear my dad's car drive up and almost instantly I hear Mami yelling for us to come into the kitchen. Every single evening, my sister and I set the table. In reality, mostly I set the table. She's always whining about stuff therefore gets away with doing nothing. No big deal, I'm used to carrying the load around here.

My dad walks in and my sister and I run towards the door to greet him. He looks tired, but always looks happy to be home. We all wash up and my mom serves dinner. You'd think I never ate a hot, cooked meal since I practically swallow all of my food instantly. My mom tells me to slow down or I will choke. My dad just laughs and says I like my mom's cooking. He's right, she does cook all of our favorite dishes from Peru and I love all of them; even the liver and onions. Most kids wouldn't be caught dead saying they liked liver and onions, but I always say, "*You would if you had my mom's*".

September 15

Dear Diary,

So today we had to choose partners in social studies so that we could do a project together. Guess who I got? Jason, the boy who gave me that note. I guess he's shy just like me since he didn't bring it up.  Come to think of it, I didn't even open it. I didn't want la chismosa Elena to find it. Tonight, after my shower, I will read it. I wonder what it says, now I can't stop thinking about it. I've never had a boyfriend, at least not a real one. Maybe this is it or maybe it isn't. Oh my – I'm definitely nervous now. Hurry up clock... tick tock... I have to read the note!

Marisol

When I get home, most of the afternoon is uneventful. I eat my snack and do my homework. I have to wash the dishes each night. The entire time I wash the dishes, my mind races about what that note might actually say. I think the blond haired boy likes me, but maybe he doesn't. I don't look anything like him. I have long curly hair and my skin is bronzed brown. He looks quite the opposite. He's white and has some weird colored eyes thing going on. While I do the dishes I start pretending I'm working in a fancy restaurant as a chef. That people are asking for me, but I'm too busy to go out to see them. I'm busy in the kitchen cooking some world-renowned dishes.

After my shower, I dry my hair as best as I can. There's so much of it, I'm afraid my arms will fall off. My mom says that if I don't dry it and I sleep with it wet I will get pneumonia and die. Sometimes I think she's exaggerating but I don't take any chances so I dry away.

I sit on my bed wishing Elena would just fall asleep. It takes her what seems like forever. She's the scaredy cat type of little sister, so it takes her a long time to settle down. She's scared of the dark, monsters, strange dogs, awkward cats, strangers, and even other family members. I can't blame her for other family members though, we have an aunt who I think is really the Wicked Witch of South America. I call her "*la bruja fea*". If my mom ever heard me call her that I'm quite certain I would have had my mouth washed out with soap or even gotten popped on the mouth! I don't want either of those to happen so I keep the rude comments to myself.

Finally, Elena falls asleep, gracias a Dios. I don't turn the light on because she might wake up. I feel under my mattress and find the note. I go into our closet and I step on the edge of my fancy church shoes! OMG it hurts so bad! I would have screamed at the top of my lungs any other time but I didn't want anyone to know I was awake so I sucked it up. I pull the little dangling string hanging from the ceiling and turn the light on. I examine my heel closely in case it looks like it could get infected, it's red, I think I'll live.

I carefully unfold the lined paper note. It's quite simple, it says:

**_Will you be my girlfriend?_**

I let out a loud gasp, too shocked to keep quiet. Well this is it, I guess I officially have a boyfriend. The first thing that pops in my mind is how will I keep this from my dad. He just wouldn't understand. I can't wait to tell Olivia, she's my best friend. She is probably the only person on this entire planet that I can tell.

I head towards the bathroom to put some rubbing alcohol on my heel. After all, I don't want it to get infected and have my foot amputated. I'm too young to be a one-foot girl.

September 19

Dear Diary,

A few days have passed since I opened the folded note Jason handed me on the bus. He has been absent so I've actually been working on our class project alone. Yes, literally all by myself. I just want to say for the record, that I am already not impressed. If he thinks I'm going to be doing all of the work just because he asked me to be his girlfriend, he has another thing coming.

What does he think this is? Besides, this isn't the 1980's why would he write me a note? Maybe he will be at school tomorrow. I hope so. I haven't even told him my answer. I am sure he will ask for my phone number.

Marisol

I decide to take a quick break before I begin my homework and see what my little brother is up to. I walk into his room and he is playing with his action figures. He's such a great little kid. If I ever have kids I want them to be just like him. He has no worries in the world. He doesn't know that my dad doesn't let us go anywhere without him and mom. He doesn't even know that we don't really have money for designer clothes. I'm glad he doesn't, I try to avoid all of that myself but it's not always easy. I stand at the doorway and just watch him.

He looks up and says, "*Come on and play with me! You can be the bad guys and I'll be the good guys!*"

Clearly, he doesn't know these characters are from different movies. Batman is not supposed to be with Superman or any of the Teenage Mutant Ninja Turtles. Oh well.

I sit down on the carpet and start playing. As I try to focus on being the bad guys, I start thinking I should borrow my mom's phone and look up Jason. I wonder if he's on social media. My friend Ana has her very own iPhone and practically lives on social media. I bet if I look on her account I will find him. Then I can look and see what he's been up to. That's really creepy, I know, but everybody does it. I think about it and *ding!* almost instantly my mom's voice pops in my head saying "*Haz bien sin mirar a quien*". That means do right without worrying about what everyone else is

11

doing. I hate when she pops in my head. I close my eyes and pray, please let it stop by the time I'm a teenager. I guess I won't stalk him… today.

September 20

Dear Diary,

Okay, so let me just say that I could not wait to get home and share all of the juicy stuff that has happened in this notebook. I can't tell my sister, remember she's la chismosa. I can't tell my mom she'd just worry about me. Of course, I cannot tell my dad, he'd kill me.

Jason came to school! I told him I read the note and after a few seconds, he looked up and smiled. I told him yes and he immediately asked if he could come over. I quickly told him that could never happen. He looked puzzled, but that's how things have to be. I'd rather he look puzzled than have to speak to my dad. I'm saving his life, he really should thank me.

Marisol

*"Marisol! We are having tallarines rojos for dinner tonight!"* Mami tells me from the kitchen.

Sweeter words could not be heard. I love my mom's spaghetti. She makes her own sauce so it's way better than the kind you buy in a can or jar. Seriously, who eats spaghetti sauce from a can? It's almost as bad as eating mashed potatoes from a box of powdered flakes. Gross!

I walk into the kitchen and it smells heavenly. Nothing could be better at this very moment...until I hear Elena...

*"Ooooh Mami look at what Marisol wrote in her diary! She has a boyfriiieeenddd!!!!"*

Am I hearing this right? Is this a nightmare? This cannot be happening to me! I run towards Elena. She starts to scream and runs around the other side of the couch. I yell at her and tell her I hate her. My mom grabs the diary, closes it and hands it back to me. She looks at me and tells me to keep it safe. She looks at Elena and tells her she should not invade my privacy.

Elena runs to the bathroom, slams the door and yells, *"Wait until daddy gets home, I'm telling on both of you!"*

# Chapter 2

# Rule #1

# Stay Away from Boys

September 20

Dear Diary,

Should I hate Elena?

Well there you have it, just when I thought there might be a small chance that Elena and I could get along, she goes and erases any of those chances. It's almost like she only exists to make my life miserable. After she told my mom and locked herself in the bathroom, I just went to my bedroom and laid on my bed. I didn't even bother getting under the covers. I might've gotten in trouble for that. My bed would look messy and my mom would not let that slide, emotional crisis or not.

I waited to be called to the kitchen as my dad arrived home. I silently prayed to the virgencita Maria that Elena would forget to tell daddy and that my mom would break her marriage vows and keep secrets from him, at least this one.

Just so you know, none of that happened...Why? Well, because the universe hates me that's why!  Elena waited until daddy got home, then ran towards the door and yelled,

*"Mari has a boyfriend!!!!"*

I looked up at Papi and he looked at me without saying a word. He told all of us to wash up and sit at the table. After we all washed up and I helped Mami set the dishes, we sat down for what normally would be my favorite part of the day- dinner. And to rub more salt in the wound, it was tallarines rojos, my most favorite dish on the planet!

18

Well, I was quiet and eventually my dad looked up and asked me what Elena was talking about. I asked permission to get the note. He nodded and I excused myself. I brought the note and told him how it all happened, except I left out all of the details of me reading it in the closet in the middle of the night. Oh, and the details of Jason and I being partners at school. He would have made sure my teacher assigned me a new partner right away. Don't get me wrong, I'm a good kid, I'm just not a saint.

Daddy listened patiently, he's kind of like that. He's not a mad dad, he's not aggressive like I hear some dads can be. He doesn't really spank us, but he's firm with us. I basically know I cannot roll my eyes at him, or talk back or say things like *"What?"* and *"Hey!"* to him. He expects a lot from all of us, including Mami, so he's not easy to talk to. Normally I don't really share with him, if I can avoid it.

But today I didn't have a choice... As I started to tell him about Jason, I kept looking at Mami. She sat quietly, nodding her head, letting me know to continue. I feel safe when she's around. She looks out for me and sticks up for me, even when I probably don't deserve it.

When I finished telling my dad how it came to be that I had a boyfriend. He paused, looked up and said, *"You don't go to school to have a boyfriend. You are not an American girl. You go to school to get an education".* He went on and on about the sacrifices he

19

made to get us into this country and how he left the car he had worked his whole life to buy just so we could come to this country. He added the fact that none of his sisters or brothers or even cousins were here as if I didn't already know how much he sacrificed.

Any time I get in any real trouble this is the same speech I receive. There is no other version of it either. This is how I know I'm in trouble. I really, really try to focus and pay attention to the entire speech, just in case he asks me something when he's done. He doesn't ever ask me anything after he delivers the speech, but  I do worry so just in case I take mental notes.

Finally, it's settled. I'm not allowed to look at boys, talk to boys, or even pretend to like boys. That shouldn't be too hard, said no 5th grader ever.

September 22

Dear Diary,

So it's been a couple of days since the "mandate" from el rey aka my dad was proclaimed. I saw Jason at school yesterday and pretended not to see him. He tried to talk to me twice, once in the hall and the other time in class as we worked on our South America project. I didn't answer either time, maybe he will quit talking to me. I don't want to get in trouble at home. Although, I think hard about what exactly it is my parents could take away from me. I don't have my own phone, I don't belong to a sports team, I am not even part of any school club. I guess they can take away my diary journal and I really can't take that chance, after all that's all I really have. Life just doesn't seem to ever be fair.

Today, the entire family is going to the beach.

These are the moments where I feel connected with my family, when I don't seem to worry about the rest of the world. I can't wait to see the beautiful ocean and feel the cool sand between my toes. I'm going to lay on my towel and pretend to be on an exotic island.

Marisol

"*Marisol!*" I hear Mami yelling for me. "*Bring your little brother and let's go!*"

"*Okay Mami*" I yell back. "*Eduardo ven ya nos vamos,*" I tell my little brother.

He looks at me, still sitting on the couch. I'm not sure if he's acting like he doesn't understand me or he really doesn't. That's one of those things that confuses me. Both my parents speak to all of us in Spanish so I don't know how he doesn't understand it. Maybe he's pretending he doesn't, so that he doesn't have to do what I tell him. I shrug and just tell him in English, "*Eduardo come on we're leaving.*"

He quickly gets up, fills his pockets with some action figures and runs out of the door, way ahead of me. I watch him running towards the car and think, this little kid is something else.

The drive to the beach is not too long. We live in Florida and we are about two hours from the coast. Mami brings a lot of fruit and drinks for our drive. During our ride, I can smell all of the yummy food that's packed. I know some people pack sandwiches and chips for a day's outing. My mom packs cooked food. I think I heard her say she made arroz con pollo, I know there's a salad, probably a cake, lots of fresh fruit and other Latino food. Another family, who are friends of my mom and dad are going too. We always go places with other people. I think my parents just like large groups and gatherings.

We get to the beach and immediately the air smells so much better. It's salty and fresh. I hear the noisy seagulls flying over our heads. I can imagine their conversation, *More people have arrived with more food, fellas!* Just like squirrels are rats with bushy tails, seagulls are the rats of the oceanside.

I help by holding Eduardo's hand and help bring the sand toys with us. That's my usual job when we are out and about- take care of Eduardo. Sometimes I have to watch Elena too. It depends if we are in a big place or not. If it's a really big place like the airport or the mall, my mom will take care of one of them, and I will watch the other.

My mom tells me to go and unpack on the seashore. I unfold the chairs, drag the toys, and set up the umbrella. I lay out the towels and help Eduardo and Elena by putting lots of sunscreen lotion on both of them. Elena is good and sits still. She doesn't like wet lotions on her, so she practically stops breathing and just stands there. Eduardo on the other hand squirms and gets more sand on him than lotion. I fuss at him, a little, and ask him to stand still. He asks me to hurry, so I give up and let him go. I watch him run towards the ocean. I just know I didn't put enough on his back and start feeling guilty right away. My mom says if we don't put enough we will get a sunburn and that hurts a lot. It will feel like a burn from the stove or something horrible like that. I run after him with his little t-shirt flowing in the air.

"*Eduardito!*" that means little Eduardo, "*Espera!*" I beg him to wait and let me put the t-shirt on him, he agrees. I kiss his little forehead and he is happy, I feel better. Is this what being a mom feels like? So weird.

As I am turning around, I look up and see a few boys playing on the shore. One looks directly at me. I don't even know what is happening, but I immediately smile at him. I immediately feel self-conscious and wonder if this stupid, old bathing suit is even cute. Why didn't I think about it before we left mi casa? I've had it for at least two years. I could have begged my mom for a new one this year. He is definitely handsome. His skin is a little bit browner than mine. He has a perfect smile and is a little taller than I am. As I walk towards Elena, who is still standing there trying to air dry, I suppose, I can feel him looking at me. I wish he'd stop. I am super embarrassed now. I tell myself not to look back towards him. I tell myself I am not an American girl, I cannot look at boys. As I finish that thought, I turn around and smile at him again.

I look up and Elena is looking at me. I can tell she's wondering what's going on.

She asks me, *"Do you know those boys?"*

I tell her no. She looks like she's not sure. I try to convince her to go up to the pavilion where the rest of

the family and friends are but she says she just wants to hang out with me. Lucky me!

I grab her hand and pick up the beach toys. We walk closer towards the shore and I dump the toys. Eduardo runs towards us, he's already wet. I tell him not to splash. He, of course, does the complete opposite. Elena yells at him and tries to throw dirt at him. I tell her to stop and to understand he's little. She frowns, the kind that she normally does when she doesn't get her way. She can be moody like that. We sit down and start building castles.

The boys start watching us. All three of them walk towards us. I almost stopped breathing. I mean, geez why would they all come. Really I mean why would he come too? Well he really can't just stay behind that would look odd. The oldest one, he must be in middle school asks if they can help. I nod and they sit down next to us. The boy who smiled at me smiles at me again. This time I just looked down. Why is he sitting next to me? Doesn't he know that's just super rude? To sit next to someone who's about to die.

They each introduce themselves. The oldest one is in middle school, he's an eighth grader, I was right! His name is Mark. The middle one is a little older too, he's in sixth grade and his name is Derrick. I like him. The youngest is four and he's totally cute. He and Eduardo are about the same age, so it's perfect. Derrick asks me how old I am, and I tell him that I'm eleven. He asks me if I'm in sixth grade too. I tell him that I'm not because when I moved to the USA, the school held me back one year. He said that was terrible, I have to agree with him.

Just when we are in the middle of the conversation, my mom walks up. She smiles and tells us es hora de comer. She asks the boys if they and their family would like to join us. Derrick runs to ask his family, there's a lot of them too, and his mom waves to us. The rest of the family smiles. His mom says, "*No, thank you*" but the boys can join us if they'd like to. All three of them say they want to join us. The entire time I wonder where Derrick goes to school.

We all get our plates and sit down on the old-looking, picnic tables. All of us sit together on one table. The music is a little loud. Derrick has to yell to tell me that my mom's arroz con pollo is delicious. I smile and tell him that I'm glad he likes Latino food. He tells me he's never met any Latino families. I like that I get to show him about what being Latino is all about. Just as I am sharing that we have music and food at every event, I look up and see my dad. He has been watching me. I immediately feel like I'm in trouble. He doesn't say anything nor does he call me over. I guess he's saving "the judgement" for later, when we get home.

I never got a chance to ask Derrick what school he went to. I think he and his family must have been visiting Florida. On the way home I kept thinking of what my dad said, that I am not an American girl and that I was not to focus on boys. In other words, focus on my education. My dad said that's Rule #1- Stay Away from Boys. I know I'm from Peru, but I'm not in Peru. It's almost like being stuck in the middle of two worlds.

In the middle of my deep thinking, I look up and see Eduardo is tired, he lays his little head on my lap. Elena is falling asleep too. I put a rolled up towel against the window and tell her to put her head there. I close my eyes. I think about how I want to make my parents proud and how I need to focus on my education.

I suddenly wake up. We are back home. I feel like I'm carrying bags of sand on me. I will rinse and head right back to sleep. I pull Eduardo's arm along into the house. I have to rinse him out too. He's a little grumpy because he's sleepy, so I pick him up. Elena is a little grumpy too, she's hanging around my mom and being whiny. So I call her towards the bathroom we three share. She comes towards us. After they are both rinsed out, they put on their pajamas and I send them to bed. I rinse myself off and soon I fall asleep too.

# Chapter 3
# Sick of Sharing

October 3

Dear Diary,

Tomorrow is Sunday, my family has to go to la iglesia. Today, I woke up super early and did my chores. Mami was not happy with the way I cleaned the bathroom. I had to do it over three times. To make things worse, when I finish my chores I then have to leave with Mami to clean some gringo's house. I am old enough so I have to clean the bathrooms in that house too.

The house is huge. I ask my mom if the man and his daughter are rich, she nods. I figured, they even have central air. We only have window air conditioners in two bedrooms. The man lives alone with his daughter, she's about my age. She doesn't speak to me when we arrive. She just looks at me and I hear her tell her dad that she doesn't want us in her room. Good! Who wants to go into her stupid room? It looks like that nasty pink stomach medicine threw up all over it.

Last Saturday, I went in her room to clean and she walked in. She found me staring at her dollhouse. Newsflash: I didn't melt it with my eyes! Geez, I was just looking.

I'm glad I don't have to clean her room. The less we have to clean the sooner we can leave. Then the rest of today can be all mine. I'm reading a good book and I can't wait to get back to it.  My dad picked us up. On our ride home, my mom said it was not good that the man said we couldn't go into his daughter's room. Mami said we need this cleaning job. She asked me if I touched anything in there. I promised her that I didn't. I can tell she didn't really believe me...

Marisol

Today I woke up super early so I can have more time to do stuff I like. Half of today will be spent getting ready for church, going to church, and then going out to eat after church. I get my backpack out and clean it out. I do this every Sunday. I hate it when it gets dirty and full of stuff I don't need. As I clean it out I find a book that I thought I lost. Phew! Now I can return it to the school librarian. She was not happy earlier this week when she asked me about it and I informed her that perhaps I had lost it. I do not want to get on her bad side, books are my only fun thing to do. It is also the only way I get to spend time by myself. When Mami asks me to do something and I tell her I'm reading she sometimes lets me just read.

As I'm finishing up, I hear Eduardo in the kitchen. I walk into the kitchen and see him sitting at the table. I ask him if he wants some cereal. He smiles and nods. He is the cutest little kid. He has morning hair. I'm pretty sure he is due for a haircut. I pour him some milk and cereal, more cereal than milk. I pour myself a bowl too. Although he likes super sweet cereal and I don't, I decided to try the cinnamon sugary stuff. I immediately regret it, I'll stick to the non-sugary stuff.

"*Buenos dias*", Mami walks into the kitchen. We both say good morning back. Mami tells me to wake up Elena and to get washed up so we can start getting ready for church. I head to my bedroom. Elena is awake, but is pretending to be asleep.

"*I know you're up Elena*", I whisper. She opens one of her eyes and frowns. She hates going to church and most of the time makes us all late. I think that's probably one of the few times I have seen my dad get mad. There's been times where she has refused to get dressed and we have gone to church anyway. Yup! Elena dressed in pajamas. To me that's more like punishing the rest of the family. She could care less, I think that's part of her mastermind evil plan— embarrass the entire family. Other times she cries and cries, so dad leaves her in the hot car. I do believe nowadays that's pretty illegal, but she still chose to stay. I mean, it's not like she's a baby, she's old enough to get up and open the door. I just know she won't. She's super stubborn. Other times she picks a fight with Eduardo, the baby. Basically she does whatever it takes to delay or just not go.

I don't really know if I like to go either. It's boring and Mami gives me a side eye if I even think of falling asleep during service or even if I look like I'm not paying attention. I sit with Eduardo on my lap and Elena on my right hand-side. It seems like the one hour service is an eternity. I do feel good about telling God my sins when I kneel down, that's about all. I'm not really a huge fan of telling the priest my mistakes. I wonder why we have to do that.

I see my aunties and their husbands there. My cousins are there too, I like seeing them. I like seeing all of them except the bruja. I am surprised she doesn't turn into flames when she walks in. I guess God is working on her so he let's her in. Another reason I've come up with is that she might be the example of who not to be.

Today Elena announces that she is not going to church because she has nothing to wear. Mami tells her not to start with her excuses and that God doesn't like malcriadas and not to make her get the chancla. I start getting ready and try to stay out of that scene. When the chancla comes out I just know it will not turn out well.

I brush my teeth and see Mami is in our bedroom. She pulls out the blue dress with the white ribbon and collar and tells Elena to put it on.

*"Actually that's my dress, Mami"*, I quickly shared.

*"Eso no importa, you have to share"*, Mom responds.

I hate having to share everything. I take care of my things. Elena does not. Why should I have to share my favorite dress with her? It's too big for her. She's going to throw a fit in my dress and probably mess it up somehow. When I grow up I'm going to have over one hundred dresses and I will not share a single one with Elena or anyone else. I hate sharing everything.

December 17

Dear Diary,

We are finally off for winter break! That means I will have some time to relax, babysit and make some money to buy some presents. I love this time of year and I love buying presents for everyone I know.

Marisol

I love the holiday break because Mami lets me sleep in a little later than usual. She is not a fan of just lazing around and sleeping all day, although I must admit that it's probably one of my most favorite pastimes in the world. It's a bit weird to have a mother who thinks the total opposite.

I hear Mami from the kitchen yell for Elena and I to wake up and get ready for the day. I cover my face with my comforter and pretend not to hear her. She knows I did, because she quickly adds she has made us banana pancakes. She knows I love those, so I get up and rub my eyes and walk to the bathroom. I look up and she smiles at me and points to my heaping plate of pancakes. Her smile lights up the room and I cannot be mad at her. I smile back at her.

As I brush my teeth, Elena just walks into the bathroom. You couldn't pay for privacy in this house. Trust me, I've tried... She begins to brush her teeth too. I wash my face and walk into the kitchen. I see a flash cross the living room, it's Eduardo. He wakes up with lots of energy. Mami calls him to sit down. I help him get in his seat.

Soon Elena joins us and we eat our pancakes, Eduardo tries to pour half of the bottle of syrup on his pancakes. Mami tells us that today we have to clean our bedrooms. That is the same thing as saying, *"Marisol clean the bedroom you and your sister share and when you're done, clean Eduardo's bedroom while he plays and pretends to help you."*

Normally, it's what I expect, but today I wanted to hang out with my friends. They're going to the mall and earlier in the week I got permission to go out. Now I know that I won't be able to go without finishing up my chores. I look up and try to remind my mom that she had already said I could go out.

She looks at me and tells me what I expected all along, "*Finish the bedrooms and then you can go*".

"*Yes Mami*," I quietly whisper as I take my last bite of pancake. As I clear my area and head to the sink to wash my cup, plate and fork, Mami tells me that I will have to take Elena with me.

Without thinking I turn around and say, "*No, I'm not taking her. Why would I?*"

I can see my response shocked her. She tries to ignore it and then tells me that Elena has to go with me or I cannot go. Ugh! I'm so tired of having to take her or Eduardo everywhere I go. I can't breathe and get a moment to myself. When I grow up I'll never have kids. I will do what I want all by myself. I won't have to ask permission or have any tag-alongs.

We arrive at Governor's Square Mall and it's crowded as usual. I like the stores there. Some are expensive so I just dream about buying something from there. Elena tags along and doesn't say much to anyone. My friend Olivia asks me if Elena is mad or something… "*Or something*".

I find the cutest sweater at a small store, I just have to try it on. I rush into the dressing room feeling amazing knowing I can use my birthday money to purchase it. I come out of the dressing room, Ta-Da... Olivia smiles and tells me right away that she loves it. She's super nice and that's why she's my BFF- best friend forever (and ever). She's a gringa, with light brown hair and doesn't know any Spanish, well she knows a few words now since I taught her some. She does like my mom's cooking which is a surprise since she normally just likes chicken nuggets.

I look over at Elena's face and she immediately has a disapproving face. She tells me that she doesn't love it and since I'll have to share it with her it's not fair that I buy this one. I want to tell her to shut up and that I had not planned to share it with her, but I think she has a point. I really do like it though I shouldn't have to choose what I can buy with my birthday money on what she likes. I guess she knows, like everyone else knows, that what I want is not really a priority. I have to share everything and it's just how it is. I go back into the dressing room and decide to leave it. It's not worth fighting over.

As we head towards the front entrance of the door, an older lady walks up to us and asks us if we decided against the sweater. I look up and tell her that I didn't want it. She asks me where I left it.

I respond, "*Hanging in the dressing room, isn't that where we are supposed to leave it?*" She stares at me like I'm being rude, but I'm staring back at her like she's being very rude. She asks us to wait a moment. I see her walking towards the dressing rooms. She looks into the room I was in and she heads back towards us. She tells us we can leave now. Elena and Olivia start walking away. I stand there and stare at the lady. She repeats herself and tells me I can leave, I just stand there looking like I don't hear her. I turn around and leave when I feel like it.

When I catch up to Olivia and Elena, they ask me what took so long. I tell them I didn't like the lady and that I wasn't ever going to buy anything from that store again. I don't think they understand and probably think I'm exaggerating, but I know I'm not.

When Papi picks us up, he asks how everything went. We all smile and say, "*fine*". I don't tell him that the lady from the store insinuated I was shoplifting and embarrassed me or how I was tired of not having a single moment in my life alone, where I could just focus on myself and be myself, basically that I'm tired of sharing. I don't tell my dad or even my mom for that matter because they both have so much to worry about. Their English is not that great, I know they're trying to make sure we pay our bills on time and have food on the table. That's why Papi works so late every day. That's why Mami babysits and cleans houses.

# Chapter 4
# Feliz Navidad

In my house Christmas (or better known as Navidad) is a month-long celebration. My mom loves the music, decorations, gatherings, and everything else that comes along with this holiday. Elena, Eduardo and I get the best of both worlds... we have an arbolito de Navidad, which we gladly decorate with our school made ornaments, Christmas stockings filled with treats, and we get to open up our presents on Christmas Eve after dinner, lots of laughing and sharing memories. We get to eat turkey, cranberry sauce and mashed potatoes right along with a roast, tamales, paneton, and arroz blanco.

December 26

Dear Diary

Christmas was so awesome for Eduardo. He got some more action figures. I was able to save some money and got him two board games. That way he won't be stuck in front of a TV or game screen. Plus, we can play together with Elena. I gave Elena a bracelet and I think she actually likes it. She's super picky and since she's so creative she has a special taste in everything. She is the hardest person to shop for. I gave my mom a lotion and my dad some socks. I had enough money to buy all of my little cousins a stuffed animal each. They were so happy to get an extra present. I just loved seeing their faces.

My Christmas was both eventful and, I have to say, loving. Elena really surprised me. She made me a card, she drew lots of hearts on it and it said I was her best friend.

I read it a few times, over and over, in my head. I thought Elena hated me. She always tells on me, but maybe I'm just not understanding her.

Marisol

# Chapter 5

# What did you say?

December 29

Dear Diary,

Today was another day where I felt the anger
inside of me build up. I'm sure it's not healthy, but
I'm not sure who to talk to or how to even bring it
up. I wish I had someone to talk to. Everyone in
my family has their own problems. I don't think
it's fair to bother any of them with my problems.
I'm sure they will think they are just kid issues.

Marisol

My mom, her sister (la bruja fea) and I went to the pharmacy. There were a few items they had to pick up and I like to tag along. Sometimes it's the only time I get to leave the house. When we got there, it smelled like medicine. It's a small family-owned pharmacy. We found almost everything on the list, except for algodón.

The lady who worked at the pharmacy was walking around and asked us if she could help us. I don't normally say anything when adults are around. I try to stay in my lane and respect that I'm to listen and not be heard. My aunt tells the lady that we are looking for cotton, but with her thick accent the lady doesn't understand. My aunt repeats it about five times. I can tell she's getting frustrated. The saleslady can see my aunt is frustrated, so she apologizes and just shakes her head to let us know they don't have the item. Again, it really doesn't sound anything close to "cotton". It sounds more like "colon" but with a double T. Ultimately, I just say, *"She wants cotton"*. The lady lights up and exclaims, *"Oh yes! We have cotton balls, follow me please"*. As we walk towards the right aisle the lady turns to me and tells me that she doesn't understand people that don't speak English. I stare back at her and pretend I too don't speak English. I'm not impressed and it certainly is not a compliment to me.

When we leave the store la bruja fea y Mami both tell me how proud they are of me. I smile. Yeah, my English is so much better than when I first arrived about a year ago. Right then and there I commit to make sure I never forget how hard it is to be new to a country. How it is not nice to make others feel bad about something they are not great at.

Oh, and la bruja fea is not mean to me. She's just mean to a lot of other people in our family. I'm not really sure why, but my mom says we should feel sorry for her. I kinda don't. I just don't like her. It's interesting that some people feel sorry for rude people and then there are those of us who just choose not to deal with those rude people. Mami says that la bruja fea has been through a lot in her life. I believe it, but I also know my own Mami has been through so much as well. When my abuelita died, my Mami had to get a job as a live-in maid for some rich people in Peru. She was not even 14 years old.

December 31

Dear Diary,

So today is the very last day of the entire year. In a few days I will be back at school and finish my last year of elementary school. I will head on to middle school. I hear it's scary there and that teachers don't care about you. I'm not too worried though, I get along with teachers. I hope the classes aren't too long.

Marisol

Mami is in the kitchen with two of her sisters. They have been cooking for the last two days. I have to make sure Eduardo goes to sleep so he won't be grumpy tonight. Vivi is thankfully entertained in our room, she got a lot of new color pencils for Christmas so she's been drawing since that day. My dress is hanging up in my closet so I check on it just to make sure it's still clean and ready for tonight.

"Marisol, la puerta," yells Mami. I quickly ran to the door to answer it. It's my mom's friend and her family from El Salvador. I kiss all of them on the cheek and call their daughter Gabriela to come to my room. She follows me. Soon everyone starts arriving, one family at a time. I wonder how everyone is fitting into our little house. I'm convinced it doesn't matter to anyone except for me. As the sun sets, the music gets a little louder, so I know the party has officially begun. I look at the clock, it's still pretty early, just a few minutes past nine o'clock.

*"Oye vengan a comer niños",* I hear someone's mom shout.

We all ran out of the room. The table is completely filled up with food. A huge turkey, tamales, empanadas, arroz, ensalada rusa, lots of vegetables, and other stuff I don't really care about. I already know there's a flan maybe two in the refrigerator and that's all I really want. After we finish, all of the moms clean up.

Mami sends me on my way and says, "*Ella me ayuda con el bebe*", She means Eduardo.

In our culture, boys are a little tiny bit spoiled (I'm being sarcastic when I say a little). So to my mom he will always be a baby. That's how I get out of washing dishes and cleaning up at family gatherings like tonight and birthday parties.

The bedroom Elena and I share is small, but somehow all of the kids at the party still fit in there. We laugh and talk about school. It would be so cool if we all went to the same school, but we don't. We live on opposite ends of the city, so my sister and I are the only Latinas at our school. When we hang out with these kids, it's pretty fun. They are all bilingual too. They are all Latinos. Their parents speak Spanish and are from other countries like Mexico, Guatemala, and Colombia. We take turns peeking outside the room. We hear the grown-ups laughing louder and louder. All of them are drinking adult beverages. We all laugh and talk about how when we visit our family's home countries kids "drink" too. That's insane! My parents don't care where we are, they still don't let me drink. I smelled beer before and it smells gross, so I am not in a rush to try it.

When it's my turn to peek at the adults, I look back and tell everyone, "*¡están bailando!*"

Immediately everyone gets up and starts dancing in the room too. Everyone but Elena, although she's probably the best dancer, she's super shy. So she won't dance even when I beg her to. She shakes her head. Eventually, we get enough confidence and decide to join the party to dance with our families. We all come out and one by one our moms and dads pull us to dance with them. It's fun, I'm having the time of my life. It's hilarious to dance with los padres because they try to give you dance lessons as you're dancing.

As I'm trying to follow my dad's lead, I turn around and I see Elena almost on the floor, holding on for her dear life and the table leg. I look up and see my uncle pulling her to the dance floor. I'm initially shocked and stunned, but quickly fall out laughing. Her face is priceless, does he not know how shy she is? I think no le importa. Ha ha ha!!!

After what seems like more time than normal, he stops pulling her. She runs to the room. I shake my head and continue dancing with my Papi. I see my friends and cousins dancing, laughing and having a great time too. I love these kinds of nights. Parties in Peru are like this too. It feels like we are in Peru just enjoying ourselves. Everyone is talking in Spanish and dancing to Latino music.

# Chapter 6

# Middle School Here I Come!

## I'm ready

March 3

Dear Diary,

I've not written in so long. Have you missed me? To be totally honest, I lost you. I couldn't find you for the life of me. I hid you so la chismosa de Elena wouldn't find you and read you. Then I forgot exactly where I hid you. Today as I spent the day cleaning I found you at the bottom of my sock drawer. I'm glad I did, there are a lot of memories here. In just a couple of months I'll be done with elementary school and I will be in middle school!

"*¿Estás lista?*" Mami asks me as she walks into my room. I'm tying my shoes.

"*Yes, I'm almost ready*", I quickly grab my purse, and head out the door with Mami. Her friend is picking us up. I smile and greet her, "*hola señora*".

I give her a hug and a kiss on her cheek. That's the way we all greet each other. It's bad manners if you don't. That's what Mami says.

"*Buenos días, Marisol*", replies Mrs. Rodriguez.

We get into her car. Elena and Eduardo don't have to come with us today. My aunt is watching them. That doesn't usually happen. It's the first time in a long time that I can recall not taking those two with us. We don't normally do anything without them. Today is a little different. We are going to buy a car. My dad doesn't know yet. I've been reading the driver's manual for the rules and telling my mom what it says in Spanish. We have been practicing for so many months. Mami finally took the written part of the test in English and passed! I am so proud of her. I think she is so proud of herself too because after she finished and she got her score she cried. *Way to go, Mami!*

Since she has to buy a car so she can practice and take the driving test, Mrs. Rodriguez offered to take us to a used car dealer. I have to go because I'm the official family interpreter. I told Olivia's dad that we were going to buy a car and he said that whatever the price on the windshield is, I have to offer a lot less. It's called negotiating and to never let them talk me into anything I don't want to pay. He also told me that if they don't treat me respectfully to leave. He said there are a lot of used car dealerships. I looked them up and he is right, there really is.

On our way there Mrs. Rodriguez says, *"It's unbelievable that you passed the test the first time"*, to my mom.

I'm proud of my mom all over again. Finally, we arrive. A man quickly walks towards us as we get out of the car. He seems nice enough. He is really skinny though and he doesn't look old enough to be selling cars, ice cream maybe, but not cars. He looks at Mrs. Rodriguez, then my mom and then me. I tell him we are looking for a car for my mom. He smiles at me and tells me there are lots of cars to choose from. I tell him we have cash and how much we want to spend. He pauses. I pause too. He tells me he's going to show us some cars.

We all follow him, once we stop at the first car I notice the price on the windshield and I tell him," *If you're going to give it to us for what I told you I wanted to spend, then that's fine,"*

He quickly walks us to some other cars. I guess he didn't believe me the first time.

We spend about half the day looking for a car and finally picking one. Mami was determined to leave with a car. She tells Mrs. Rodriguez that she can leave. I guess that means we are driving that new car home. Mrs. Rodriguez looks a little worried. She asks me if I'm okay. I tell her we will be fine. I smile to make her feel better.

That's exactly what happens, we buy the car and drive the car home. I think it took longer than walking since my mom was so nervous. Even though it took a long time, I am still proud of Mami.

May 22

Dear Diary

Today when Elena got home from school I found her in my backpack. I yelled at her, *Elena, ¿Qué estás haciendo?* I know I shocked her, because I could see it all over her face. She ran to the kitchen, where it's safe because Mami is there. I looked in my backpack to see if there was something missing, but instead I found a kid-made bookmark. Hmm... Elena knows how much I love to read and sees me taking the free bookmarks from the library. She's sweet and naughty all at the same time.

Well, school is officially over in two weeks. I'm headed to middle school. I am both excited and scared. This summer I have a list of things I want to do:

Summer List:

1. Visit the park pool
2. Go to the library and grab some more books
3. Clean out my closet
4. Babysit
5. Buy some stuff for my middle school locker
6. Teach Eduardo how to read
7. Spend more time with Elena

8. Talk Mami and Papi into letting me stay up a little later in middle school

*Marisol*

Mami if I do extra chores this summer can I get a new bathing suit? I practiced asking Mami for a new bathing suit.

I know what she's going to ask me, *"Do you need one?"* I think my old one still fits me, but I like new ones. Besides, I'm a middle schooler now. I want to wear a grown-up one. I just know my dad won't let me buy a two-piece bathing suit, even though all of the girls at my school talked about how they have one. I know what my dad will say, *"No eres Americana"*.

As I'm thinking about how to ask and the answers I need to have, Mami walks into the kitchen where I'm sitting by the counter. I tell her that I am babysitting this summer so I can buy a new bathing suit. She tells me that it's a great idea. There, I solved it.

I'm sure my dad won't let me buy just any bathing suit, I'll still have to follow his rules. That's fine, it's called compromise. I don't dare buy a two-piece and hide it. If I do, with my luck, he will find it or you know who will tell on me. So I don't chance it. I choose my battles.

*"Elena, I'm going to the mall, do you want to go?"*

She quickly says, *"Yes! I want to go".*

I smile. Yeah she gets on my nerves sometimes, but I love her. Afterall she's my little sister and I think that her job is to annoy me.

My mom drops us off and doesn't make me take Eduardo with us. Phew! Elena and I buy ice cream and walk throughout the mall. We try on clothes and dream of being able to buy all of those outfits. I pick out a cute top, some earrings and a new pair of jeans. Elena gets to pick out an outfit too. I have saved money from babysitting. I don't buy a new bathing suit after all. The old one still fits and it's cute enough.  I guess my mom would say I'm growing up, and learning to make good decisions.


Middle School Here I Come!

# Meet the Author

***Nury Castillo Crawford*** is a first generation immigrant. Her stories are snippets into her childhood as she transitioned into a new culture in the USA. For Nury, writing her own version of immigration via the lens of a child is both personal and of the utmost importance. "It is so important for all children to see themselves in the books they read." As our country's diversity grows, so does the importance of books such as these.

Nury is also an educator and has found her calling in supporting children of all ages find strength in who they are. She currently lives in Metro Atlanta, loves to travel, and is an advocate for her community.

Her first book was published in 2017, ***3,585 Miles to be an American Girl***. This book is the first in her bilingual books series. It follows a little girl as she arrives in the USA and tries to find her way filled with lots of triumphs and even some challenges along the way. Nury is active on social media and loves to interact with book lovers, educators and writers too!

Other books by Nury Castillo Crawford:

3,585 Miles to be an American Girl (Bilingual English/Spanish)

Sofia and Vivi: Big Sister  (Bilingual English/Spanish)

Plant the Seed Well, Expect Wonders (English)

Siembra bien la semilla, Cosecha maravillas (Spanish)

A Long Journey to Safety (co-author, Vietnamese and English)

What Is Going On In The World? (Bilingual English/Spanish)

# Meet the Illustrator

***Demitrius Motion Bullock***, artist, illustrator, has amassed a portfolio of work that includes a number of logo creations and designs for a wide variety of industries. He has illustrated over 22 publications to date which include book cover designs for a number of independent book authors, children's books and comic book illustrations.

As a self-taught artist from the Bronx, NY in multiple mediums, he was inspired by early street artists he witnessed as a child. Along with his fascination with comic and graphic art has led him to develop several of his own characters.

In addition to the 4 other titles he's worked on with Nury and 1010 Publishing, he continues drawing and creating his own artwork and the building of his business Motion Illustrationz with his wife, Michelle and son, Bryce. Follow him on Instagram @ Demitrius_Motion_Bullock, and www.motionillustrationz.com.

Made in the USA
Columbia, SC
23 January 2021